For Timmy, Ma and Essie xxx
– S.B.

Bloomsbury Publishing, London, New Delhi, New York and Sydney

First published in Great Britain in 2014 by Bloomsbury Publishing Plc
50 Bedford Square, London, WC1B 3DP

This paperback edition first published in 2015

A CIP catalogue record of this book is available from the British Library

ISBN 978 1 4088 3921 8 (HB)
ISBN 978 1 4088 3922 5 (PB)
ISBN 978 1 4088 3923 2 (eBook)

Printed in China by C&C Offset Printing Co Ltd, Shenzhen, Guangdong

1 3 5 7 9 10 8 6 4 2

All papers used by Bloomsbury Publishing are natural, recyclable products made
from wood grown in well-managed forests. The manufacturing processes conform
to the environmental regulations of the country of origin

www.bloomsbury.com

BLOOMSBURY is a registered trademark of Bloomsbury Publishing Plc

The Dawn Chorus

Suzanne Barton

BLOOMSBURY

LONDON NEW DELHI NEW YORK SYDNEY

Deep in the forest, the trees rustled and the animals stirred. The day had just begun.

Perched on his branch, Peep woke
to the sound of a beautiful song.
"Who's that singing?" he wondered.

Peep stretched out his wings,
fluffed up his feathers . . .

And decided to follow the tune.

He soared on the breeze to the
edge of the forest, where, high
up in a tree, he found an owl.

"Is it you who's singing?" asked Peep.
"It's not me," hooted the owl.

So Peep glided down to the field below, weaving
through the corn. And soon he spotted a mouse.

"Is that your wonderful
song?" said Peep.

"It's not me," squeaked the mouse.

Peep hopped through the poppies and followed
the song down to the riverbank. As he watched
the water sparkle and swirl, up popped a frog.

"Have you been singing?"
said Peep.

"No!" croaked the frog. "The song
is coming from over there . . ."

Peep looked up and saw an enormous tree on the top of a hill. The tree was full of birds and they were all singing! Peep landed on one of the branches and listened.

"That was beautiful!" said Peep when they had finished. "I've never heard anything so lovely."

"Thank you!" chirped a friendly bird. "We're the Dawn Chorus."

"What's the Dawn Chorus?" Peep asked.

"We sing together each morning," said the bird.
"Our song lets everyone know that it's the
start of a new day."

Peep thought for a moment.
"Can I sing with you? Please?"

"Come for an audition tomorrow,"
said the conductor. "We start at dawn."

Peep was so excited that he
flew straight home . . .

And practised all evening.

And when he couldn't sing
another note, he fell fast asleep.

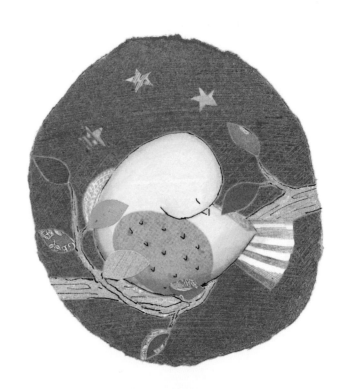

The next morning he awoke in a panic.

"You're going to be late for your audition!" called Owl.

Peep blinked his sleepy eyes in the bright sunshine.
"Oh no!" he cried, and he flew off as fast as he could.

But he was too late.

"I'm sorry, Peep. The day has begun
– the Dawn Chorus has already sung,"
said the conductor.

"Can I have one more chance?"
begged Peep.

"Come back tomorrow," said the conductor. "But you mustn't be late!"

That day, Peep practised and practised.
He sang so sweetly that all of the forest
animals stopped to listen.

The hours passed and Peep felt very tired,
but he wouldn't go to sleep – he didn't
want to miss his audition again.

He watched the
stars as night fell.

Just before dawn, Peep set off for the
audition. But when he got there, he
was so tired that all he could do was . . .

YAWN!

"Oh dear, Peep," the conductor sighed.
"Perhaps you're just not meant to sing."

Peep felt very sad as he walked away.
"Now I'll never be part of the Dawn
Chorus," he said to himself.

He flew home all alone. And as the
sun started to set, he sang softly.

After a while, Peep heard another sweet
song drifting towards him and, not far away,
he saw a bird who looked just like him.

"Why can I sing in the evening," asked Peep,
"but not in the morning with the Dawn Chorus?"

"Because you're a nightingale, just
like me," said the bird.
"Nightingales don't sing at dawn,
they sing at night!"

And so, as the stars came out and the moon shone brightly, the two nightingales sang the most beautiful song of all.

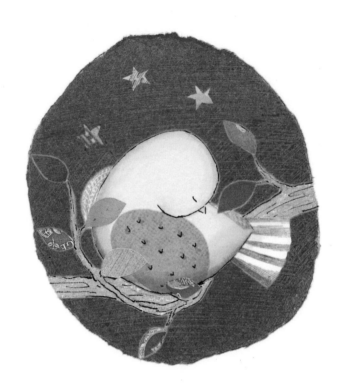